DRUMBEATS

KEVIN J. ANDERSON • NEIL PEART

Special Edition

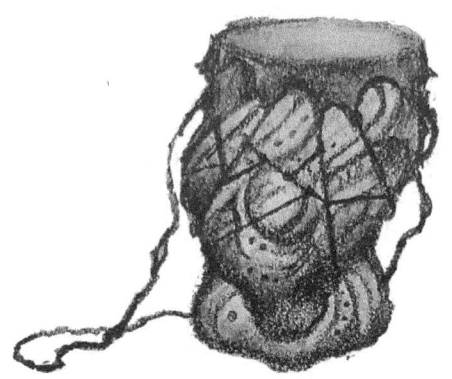

DRUMBEATS
Special Edition

Kevin J. Anderson & Neil Peart
Copyright © 2020 WordFire, Inc. and Pratt Music
First published in *Shock Rock II*, ed. Jeff Gelb, Pocket Books, 1994
Illustrations copyright © 2020 Steve Otis

All rights reserved. No part of this book may be reproduced or transmitted in any form or by any electronic or mechanical means, including photocopying, recording or by any information storage and retrieval system, without the express written permission of the copyright holder, except where permitted by law. This novel is a work of fiction. Names, characters, places and incidents are either the product of the author's imagination, or, if real, used fictitiously.

Hardback ISBN: 978-1-68057-129-5
Trade Paperback ISBN: 978-1-68057-127-1
eBook ISBN: 978-1-68057-128-8
Cover and interior artwork by Steve Otis
Cover design by Janet McDonald
Interior design by Allyson Longueira

Kevin J. Anderson, Art Director
Published by
WordFire Press, LLC
PO Box 1840
Monument, CO 80132
Kevin J. Anderson & Rebecca Moesta, Publishers
Printed in the USA
Join our WordFire Press Readers Group for
sneak previews, updates, new projects, and giveaways.
Sign up at wordfirepress.com

CONTENTS

Foreword: Mystic Rhythms—Kevin J. Anderson	1
Drumbeats	17
Afterword: Stories to Fire My Imagination—Neil Peart	55
About the Authors	67
About the Artist	71
Acknowledgments	73
If You Liked...	75

FOREWORD: MYSTIC RHYTHMS

KEVIN J. ANDERSON

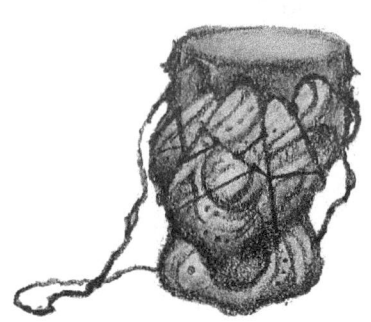

THE LETTER CAME ON A BAD DAY.

I was working as a technical writer for the Lawrence Livermore National Laboratory, where I produced respirator safety manuals and chemical protective clothing handbooks. I had to deal with DOE regulations, editing the commas in health and safety codes, going to meetings, compiling annual reports, and delivering rush presentations.

I had always dreamed of becoming an author, but this wasn't what I'd had in mind. At least I spent my evenings and weekends working on my novels.

The real-world tech-editor job offered plenty of challenges, problems, and chances to screw up. On that particular day I had been hit from several sides: An important annual report, produced by me, was released to great fanfare ... and somehow the author's name was *misspelled* on the title page. Also, I had put together a very important rush presentation on laser technology, while the anxious researcher was waiting to race off to Washington, DC to beg for continued funding; but when the slides came out of the photo lab, somehow the techs had printed all the photos *upside down*, and there was no time to fix it.

The biggest blow came from another direction. This was the day that one of the largest and most important magazines in my field, *Asimov's Science Fiction*, ran a review of my second novel, *Gamearth*. It was my first major review in a national market, distributed to all my professional peers ... and the reviewer tore me to shreds.

So, it was not a good day.

Sullen, I came home to my little townhouse in Livermore, California. I was just a single guy hoping to make a living as a writer someday. I'd published a handful of short stories and two paperback novels for minor advances, but nobody knew my name. Bummed, I got the mail, sorted through the bills, the grocery flyers, the junk mail.

And I found an envelope with a Canadian stamp. The return address said N. Peart.

My heart skipped a beat. It couldn't possibly ...

I opened the letter to find a three-page single-spaced letter from Neil Peart, legendary drummer and lyricist for the rock band Rush. A man whose work I had admired since my high school days. He had written to tell me how much he loved my first novel, *Resurrection, Inc.*

It was no longer a bad day.

Now, this wasn't entirely a coincidence. My novel, published by Signet Books in 1988, had been greatly inspired by the Rush album *Grace Under Pressure* [1984]. When I received my first author copies of the garish paperback with a hideous-looking cover (complete with stone skull and rocket ship), I autographed copies to the three members of Rush, acknowledging their influence on the work, and mailed the package off to Mercury Records, where I assumed the envelope just went into a warehouse similar to where the Ark of the Covenant is stored. Since so much time had passed, I'd forgotten about it and no longer expected any response.

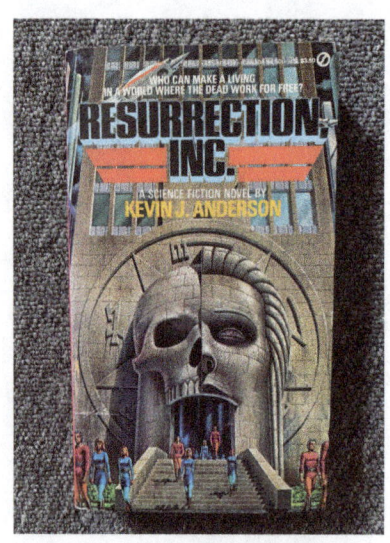

In the letter, Neil wrote, "It has taken a year, but at last I can write to you and tell you that your book did indeed make it to me. Yes—I might have written *earlier* with that information, but now, finally, I can also say that I have *read* it. Just as you could only hope that your message would make it through all the intermediary barriers to me, so too do I hope that this delinquent response will actually make it to *you*."

Well, it did, and it made my day.

"I have finally *read* it. Just finished it last night. And more importantly, I thought it was very, very good. More about that later …"

As a science fiction nerd, I have been attracted to Rush music since my teenage years with their epic fantasy songs, science fiction dystopias, space adventures—the lyrics were all so fundamentally different from the usual "Ooh baby baby" pablum on the radio. I was a skinny kid with a bad haircut, thick glasses, and hand-me-down clothes. I had no experience with girlfriends, so love songs did not resonate, but I did read a lot of books. And Rush music spoke to me.

Grace Under Pressure came at exactly the right time, when I was developing my first novel, and the lyrics fired my imagination. I wrote *Resurrection,*

Inc. with the album playing over and over, and the images conjured by the songs made their way into the story.

When the paperback was published, I wrote a dedication, right up front, "To Neal Peart, Geddy Lee, and Alex Lifeson of RUSH, whose haunting album *Grace Under Pressure* inspired much of this novel." (Yes, shudder, I actually misspelled Neil's name.)

Neil wrote, "Regarding your dedication to the humble members of Rush, needless to say I am pleased and flattered by it, but I think you do yourself a disservice by saying that your work was even partly inspired by the songs of *Grace Under Pressure*. (Though since I consider that to be one of our most underappreciated albums, I am glad to see it get some attention, however undeserved. And your description of it as 'haunting' is one of the highest compliments, in my view, that can be attached to a work of art.)

"I loved the echoes of 'Red Sector A' and 'The Enemy Within' which you wove into your story, but apart from that you have gone so far beyond anything I have experienced in lyrics that the dedication seems unmerited.

"Never mind—it's still a very nice thing, and I'm proud of it."

DRUMBEATS

Best of all, at the bottom of the letter, he added a little P.S. that I took to heart.

Yours Truly,
Neil Peart

P.S. — If you care to correspond, I would be glad to hear from you.

Neil and I began corresponding, and we immediately clicked. This was in the days before quick email exchanges—no, Neil and I wrote full-on *letters*, many pages long, each one an epic missive. I once teased him for going on at "Peartian lengths," an adjective that he took to heart and repeated in other correspondence.

I loved to hike. He loved to bicycle long distance. I would describe for him my mountain trips, my expeditions in Death Valley. I sent him a photo from the summit of Telescope Peak in Death Valley, a magical place with a unique perspective. In one direction, you can see Badwater Basin, the lowest point in the continental US (279 feet below sea level), and in another direction you can see Mount Whitney (14,505 ft), the highest point in the continental US.

(Much later, after many personal tragedies, Neil went to Telescope Peak himself and used that metaphor in his lyrics for the song "Ghost Rider"—*"from the lowest low to the highest high."*)

Neil himself took several amazing trips, and they seem unbelievable to me now. He would depart for Africa with his bicycle and go off by himself on dirt roads through the wildest country and the poorest villages, trying to speak the language, communicating with smiles and hand gestures, sometimes talking his way through armed guards at checkpoints. There he was, a famous rock drummer on a bicycle, just experiencing Africa.

"During the past few years, I have become increasingly interested in prose writing myself, and have been slowly trying to 'train' myself in the art of expressing thoughts and feelings in 'good' writing. Nothing so ambitious as your undertaking; so far I have limited myself to attempting to describe some of my travels; to put into words the experiences and impressions of my adventures in China, Africa, and on different cycling expeditions. Not aiming for publication as yet, but simply as exercises, as good training ground for learning how to use words. My apprenticeship, as it were."

And what an apprenticeship!

His descriptions were incredible. He went on for paragraphs about African villages he had visited, people he had met, adventures he'd had, and a unique African drum he had purchased from a village artisan. As part of one expedition he'd even climbed Mount Kilimanjaro, chronicling the grueling days-long hike from sea level all the way up to 19,308 feet. He mocked the tourist brochure that blithely claimed, "Any reasonably healthy adult can do it."

Eventually, Neil put together his experiences around the Kilimanjaro climb in a little self-published book, *The African Drum*. I helped him with some layout advice, which was what I did in my day job for the Livermore Lab, and he printed up a small number of copies for friends and family. (*The African Drum* remains one of my most precious treasures.)

Off and on, Neil and I had mused about collaborating on something, possibly lyrics (but I am by no means a poet), though we never found a realistic project that worked for both of us.

Then in 1993, editor Jeff Gelb invited me to contribute a story to an anthology he was putting together, *Shock Rock II*—horror/dark fantasy stories with a rock music theme. I immediately thought of a creepy adventure modeled on Neil's experiences in isolated Africa and some of the strange villages he had encountered. Hmmm, I could pull generously from the descriptions and landscapes that Neil written about his real travels, vivid and colorful details that I would never be able to pull off on my own. I suggested to Neil that I would write the actual story with a setting painted from his words, and we'd call it a collaboration. He was excited by the idea, and when I asked Jeff Gelb if he would like a story coauthored with the drummer from Rush, he responded with a dubious letter asking me to prove that I really knew Neil Peart (!).

I worked on the draft of "Drumbeats," developing the plotline and the characters, which was my forte,

and layering in the rich, sensory details of the setting, which was Neil's forte. Neil enjoyed working over the draft and sending it back to me.

Shock Rock II was published by Pocket Books in 1994, and when I sent Neil his half of the $250 payment (a very reasonable professional rate), he responded jokingly, "I guess I won't quit drumming anytime soon."

And I'm glad he didn't. Neil invited me backstage to every Rush concert tour since 1990.

The response to "Drumbeats" was very favorable, and the story was reprinted several times. In 2005, I asked Neil to write the introduction to one of my collections, *Landscapes*, and he graciously agreed, but our greatest collaboration began in 2011, when he asked for my brainstorming help for a new concept album he was developing, a steampunk fantasy adventure, *Clockwork Angels*.

Our novel version of *Clockwork Angels* became a *New York Times* bestseller and won the Scribe Award. We wrote a second novel in that universe, *Clockwork Lives*, which won the Colorado Book Award and (even more meaningful to me) Neil deemed it, "surely your finest work."

Many fans kept asking about our story "Drumbeats" and scoured used bookstores for *Shock Rock II* or other places where the story had been reprinted. We decided to put it up as an e-story, with a new Afterword by Neil. That version was available for those who just wanted the text.

For years we talked about releasing an expanded, illustrated print edition, convinced that we would always "get around to it." We also did a lot of development work on a third Clockwork novel, *Clockwork Destiny*, which remains unfinished. Each time we saw each other, we talked about the third novel, but it was never to be, at least not in Neil's lifetime ... and we both knew it.

The *Clockwork Angels* album, which *Classic Rock* magazine dubbed the greatest rock album of the decade, was the last studio album from Rush.

Neil Peart died after a long battle with brain cancer on January 7, 2020. He was my coauthor on two novels, two graphic novels, and this short story. He was my friend for more than thirty years. And he was, and is, my inspiration for most of my life.

—Kevin J. Anderson

DRUMBEATS

DRUMBEATS

AFTER NINE MONTHS OF TOURING ACROSS NORTH America—with hotel suites and elaborate dinners and clean sheets every day—it felt good to be hot and dirty, muscles straining not for the benefit of any screaming audience, but just to get to the next village up the dusty road, where none of the natives recognized Danny Imbro or knew his name. To them, he was just another White Man, an exotic object of awe for little children, a target of scorn for drunken soldiers at border checkpoints.

Bicycling through Africa was about the furthest thing from a rock concert tour that Danny could imagine—which was why he did it, after promoting the latest Blitzkrieg album and performing each song until the tracks were worn smooth in his head. This cleared his mind, gave him a sense of balance, perspective.

The other members of Blitzkrieg did their own thing during the group's break months. Phil, whom they called the "music machine" because he couldn't stop writing music, spent his relaxation time cranking out film scores for Hollywood; Reggie caught up on his reading, soaking up grocery bags full of political thrillers and mysteries; Shane turned into a vegetable on Maui. But Danny Imbro took his expensive-but-battered bicycle and bummed around West Africa. The others thought it strangely appropriate that the band's drummer would go off hunting for tribal rhythms.

Late in the afternoon on the sixth day of his ride through Cameroon, Danny stopped in a large open market and bus depot in the town of Garoua. The marketplace was a line of mud-brick kiosks and chophouses, the air filled with the smell of baked dust and stones, hot oil and frying beignets. Abandoned cars squatted by the roadside, stripped clean but unblemished by corrosion in the dry air. Groups of men and children in long blouses like nightshirts idled their time away on the street corners.

Wives and daughters appeared on the road with their buckets, going to fetch water from the well on the other side of the marketplace. They wore bright-colored *pagnes* and kerchiefs, covering their traditionally naked breasts with T-shirts or castoff Western blouses, since the government in the capital city of Yaoundé had forbidden women from going topless.

Behind one kiosk in the shade sat a pan holding several bottles of Coca-Cola, Fanta, and ginger ale, cooling in water. Some vendors sold a thin stew of bony fish chunks over gritty rice, others sold *fufu*, a doughlike paste of pounded yams to be dipped into a sauce of meat and okra. Bread merchants stacked their long *baguettes* like dry firewood.

Danny used the back of his hand to smear sweat-caked dust off his forehead, then removed the bandanna he wore under his helmet to keep the sweat out of his eyes. With streaks of white skin peeking through the layer of grit around his eyes, he probably looked like some strange lemur.

In halting French, he began haggling with a wiry boy to buy a bottle of water. Hiding behind his kiosk, the boy demanded 800 francs for the water, an outrageous price. While Danny attempted to bargain it down, he saw the gaunt, grayish-skinned man walking through the marketplace like a wind-up toy running down.

The man was playing a drum.

The boy cringed and looked away. Danny kept staring. The crowd seemed to shrink away from the strange man as he wandered among them, continuing his incessant beat. He wore his hair long and unruly, which in itself was unusual among the close-cropped Africans. In the equatorial heat, the long, stained overcoat he wore must have heated his body like a furnace, but the man did not seem to notice. His eyes were focused on some invisible distance.

"*Huit-cent francs,*" the boy insisted on his price, holding the lukewarm bottle of water just out of Danny's reach.

The staggering man walked closer, tapping a slow monotonous beat on the small cylindrical drum under his arm. He did not change his tempo but continued to play as if his life depended on it. Danny saw that the man's fingers and wrists were wrapped with scraps of hide; even so, he had beaten his fingertips bloody.

Danny stood transfixed. He had heard tribal musicians play all manner of percussion instruments, from hollowed tree trunks, to rusted metal cans, to beautifully carved *djembe* drums with goat-skin drumheads—but he had never heard a tone so rich and sweet, with such an odd echoey quality as this strange African drum.

In the studio, he had messed around with drum synthesizers and reverbs and the new technology designed to turn computer hackers into musicians. But this drum sounded different, solid and pure, and it hooked him through the heart, hypnotizing him. It distracted him entirely from the unpleasant appearance of its bearer.

"What is that?" he asked.

"Sept-cent francs," the boy insisted in a nervous whisper, dropping his price to 700 and pushing the water closer.

Danny walked in front of the staggering man, smiling broadly enough to show the grit between his teeth, and listened to the tapping drumbeat. The drummer turned his gaze to Danny and stared through him. The pupils of his eyes were like two gaping bullet wounds through his skull. Danny took a step backward but found himself moving to the beat. The drummer faced him, finding his audience. Danny tried to place the rhythm, to burn it into his mind—something this mesmerizing simply had to be included in a new Blitzkrieg song.

Danny looked at the cylindrical drum, trying to determine what might be causing its odd double-resonance—a thin inner membrane, perhaps? He saw nothing but elaborate carvings on the sweat polished wood, and a drumhead with a smooth, dark-brown coloration. He knew the Africans used all kinds of skin for their drumheads, and he couldn't begin to guess what this was.

He mimed a question to the drummer, then asked, *"Est-ce-que je peux l'essayer?"* May I try it?

The gaunt man said nothing, but held out the drum near enough for Danny to touch it without interrupting his obsessive rhythm. His overcoat flapped open, and the hot stench of decay made Danny stagger backward, but he held his ground, reaching for the drum.

Danny ran his fingers over the smooth drumskin, then tapped with his fingers. The deep sound resonated with a beat of its own, like a heartbeat. It delighted him. "For sale? *Est-ce-que c'est a vendre?*" He took out a thousand francs as a starting point, although if water alone cost 800 francs here, this drum was worth much, much more.

The man snatched the drum away and clutched it to his chest, shaking his head vigorously. His drumming hand continued its unrelenting beat.

Danny took out two thousand francs, then was disappointed to see not the slightest change of expression

on the odd drummer's face. "Okay, then, where was the drum made? Where can I get another one? *Où est-ce qu'on peut trouver un autre comme ça?*" He put most of the money back into his pack, keeping 200 francs out. Danny stuffed the money into the fist of the drummer; the man's hand seemed to be made of petrified wood. "*Où?*"

The man scowled, then gestured behind him, toward the Mandara Mountains along Cameroon's border with Nigeria. "*Kabas.*"

He turned and staggered away, still tapping on his drum as if to mark his footsteps. Danny watched him go, then returned to the kiosk, unfolding the map from his pack. "Where is this Kabas? Is it a place? *C'est un village?*"

"*Huit-cent francs,*" the boy said, offering the water again at his original 800 franc price.

Danny bought the water, and the boy gave him directions.

He spent the night in a Garouan hotel that made Motel 6 look like Caesar's Palace. Anxious to be on his way to find his own new drum, Danny roused a local vendor and cajoled him into preparing a quick omelet for breakfast. He took a sip from his 800 franc bottle of water, saving the rest for the long bike ride, then pedaled off into the stirring sounds of early morning.

As Danny left Garoua on the main road, heading toward the mountains, savanna and thorn trees stretched away under a crystal sky. A pair of doves bathed in the dust of the road ahead, but as he rode toward them, they flew up into the last of the trees with a *chuk-chuk* of alarm and a flash of white tail feathers. Smoke from grassfires on the plains tainted the air.

How different it was to be riding through a landscape, he thought—with no walls or windows between his senses and the world—rather than just riding by it. Danny felt the road under his thin wheels, the sun, the wind on his body. It made a strange place less exotic, yet it became infinitely more real.

The road out of Garoua was a wide boulevard that turned into a smaller road heading north. With his bicycle tires humming and crunching on the irregular pavement, Danny passed a few ragged cotton fields, then entered the plains of dry, yellow grass and thorny scrub, everywhere studded with boulders and sculpted anthills. By 7:30 in the morning, a hot breeze rose, carrying a honeysuckle-like perfume. Everything vibrated with heat.

Within an hour, the road grew worse, but Danny kept his pace, taking deep breaths in the trance-like state that kept the horizon moving closer. Drums. Kabas. Long rides helped him clear his head, but he found he had to concentrate to steer around the worst ruts and the biggest stones.

Great columns of stone appeared above the hills to east and west. One was pyramid-shaped, one a huge rounded breast, yet another a great stone phallus. Danny had seen photographs of these "inselberg" formations caused by volcanoes that had eroded over the eons, leaving behind vertical cores of lava.

Erosion had struck the road here too, turning it into a heaving washboard, which then veered left into a trough between tumbled boulders and up through a gauntlet of thorn trees. Danny stopped for another drink of water, another glance at the map. The water boy at the kiosk had marked the location of Kabas with his fingernail, but it was not printed on the map.

After Danny had climbed uphill for an hour, the beaten path became no more than a worn trail, forcing him to squeeze between walls of thorns and dry millet stalks. The squadrons of hovering dragonflies were harmless, but the hordes of tiny flies circling his face were maddening, and he couldn't pedal fast enough to escape them.

It was nearly noon, the sun reflecting straight up from the dry earth, and the little shade cast by the scattered trees dwindled to a small circle around the trunks. "Where the hell am I going?" he said to the sky.

But in his head, he kept hearing the odd, potent beat resonating from the bizarre drum he had seen in the Garoua marketplace. He recalled the grayish, shambling man who had never once stopped tapping on his drum, even though his fingers bled. No matter how bad the road got, Danny thought, he would keep going. He'd never been so intrigued by a drumbeat before, and he never left things half-finished.

Danny Imbro was a goal-oriented person. The other members of Blitzkrieg razzed him about it, that once he made up his mind to do something, he plowed ahead, defying all common sense. Back in school, he had made up his mind to be a drummer. He had hammered away at just about every object in sight with his fingertips, pencils, silverware, anything that made noise. He kept at it until he drove everyone else around him nuts, and somewhere along the line he became good.

Now people stood at the chain link fences behind concert halls and applauded whenever he walked from the backstage dressing rooms out to the tour buses—as if he were somehow doing a better job of walking than any of them had ever seen before....

Up ahead, an enormous buttress tree, a gnarled and twisted pair of trunks hung with cable-thick vines, cast a wide patch of shade. Beneath the tree, watching him approach, sat a small boy.

The boy leaped to his feet, as if he had been waiting for Danny. Shirtless and dusty, he held a hooklike, withered arm against his chest; but his grin was completely disarming. "*Je suis guide?*" the boy called.

Relief stifled Danny's laugh. He nodded vigorously. "*Oui!*" Yes, he could certainly use a guide right about now. "*Je cherche Kabas—village des tambours.* The village of drums."

The smiling boy danced around like a goat, jumping from rock to rock. He was pleasant-faced and healthy looking, except for the crippled arm; his skin was very dark, but his eyes had a slight Asian cast. He chattered in a high voice, a mixture of French and native dialect. Danny caught enough to understand that the boy's name was Anatole.

Before the boy led him on, though, Danny dismounted, leaning his bicycle against a boulder, and unzipped his pack to take out the raisins, peanuts, and the dry remains of a baguette. Anatole watched him with wide eyes, and Danny gave him a handful of raisins, which the boy wolfed down. Small flies whined around their faces as they ate. Danny answered the boy's incessant questions with as few words as possible: did he come from America, did black boys live there, why was he visiting Cameroon?

The short rest sank its soporific claws into him, but Danny decided not to give in. An afternoon siesta made a lot of sense, but now that he had his own personal guide to the village, he made it his goal not to stop again until they reached Kabas. "Okay?" Danny raised his eyebrows and struggled to his feet.

Anatole sprang out from the shade and fetched Danny's bike for him, struggling with one arm to keep it upright. After several trips to Africa, Danny had seen plenty of withered limbs, caused by childhood diseases, accidents, and bungled inoculations. Out here in the wilder areas, such problems were even more prevalent, and he wondered how Anatole managed to survive; acting as a "guide" for the rare travelers would hardly suffice.

DRUMBEATS

Danny pulled out a hundred francs—an eighth of what he had paid for one bottle of water—and handed it to the boy, who looked as if he had just been handed the crown jewels. Danny figured he had probably made a friend for life.

Anatole trotted ahead, gesturing with his good arm. Danny pedaled after him.

The narrow valley captured a smear of greenness in the dry hills, with a cluster of mango trees, guava trees, and strange baobabs with eight-foot-thick trunks. Playing the knowledgeable tour guide, Anatole explained that the local women used the baobab fruits for baby formula if their breast milk failed. The villagers used another tree to manufacture an insect repellent.

The houses of Kabas blended into the landscape, because they were of the landscape—stones and branches and grass. The walls were made of dry mud, laid on a handful at a time, and the roofs were thatched into cones. Tiny pink and white stones studded the mud, sparkling like quartz in the sun.

At first the place looked deserted, but then an ancient man emerged from a turret-shaped hut. An enormous cutlass dangled from his waist, although the shrunken man looked as if it might take him an hour just to lift the blade. Anatole shouted something, then gestured for Danny to follow him. The great cutlass swayed against the old man's unsteady knees as he bowed slightly—or stooped—and greeted Danny in formal, unpracticed French. *"Bonsoir!"*

"Makonya," Danny said, remembering the local greeting from Garoua. He walked his bike in among the round and square buildings. A few chickens scratched in the dirt, and a pair of black-and-brown goats nosed between the huts. A sinewy, long-limbed old woman wearing only a loincloth tended a fire. He immediately started looking for the special drums but saw none.

Within the village, a high-walled courtyard enclosed two round huts. Gravel covered the open area between them, roofed over with a network of serpent-shaped sticks supporting grass mats. This seemed to be the chief's compound. Anatole held Danny's arm and dragged him forward.

Inside the wall, a white-robed figure reclined in a canvas chair under an acacia tree. His handsome features had a North African cast, thin lips over white teeth, and a rakish mustache. His aristocratic head was wrapped in a red-and-white checked scarf, and even in repose he was obviously tall. He looked every bit the romantic desert prince, like Rudolf Valentino in *The Sheik*. After greeting Danny in both French and the local language, the chief gestured for his visitor to sit beside him.

Before Danny could move, two other boys appeared carrying a rolled-up mat of woven grass, which they spread out for him. Anatole scolded them for horning in on his customer, but the two boys cuffed him and ignored his protests. Then the chief shouted at them all for disturbing his peace and drove the boys away. Danny watched them kicking Anatole as they scampered away from the chief, and he felt for his new friend, angry at how tough people picked on weaker ones the world over.

He sat cross-legged on the mat, and it took him only a moment to begin reveling in the moment of relaxation. No cars or trucks disturbed the peace. He was miles from the nearest electricity, or glass window, or airplane. He sat looking up into the leaves of the acacia, listening to the quiet buzz of the villagers, and thought, "I'm living in a *National Geographic* documentary!"

Anatole stole back into the compound, bearing two bottles of warm Mirinda orange soda, which he gave to Danny and the chief. Other boys gathered under the tree, glaring at Anatole, then looking at Danny with ill-concealed awe.

After several moments of polite smiling and nodding, Danny asked the chief if all the boys were his children. Anatole assisted in the unnecessary translation.

"*Oui,*" the chief said, patting his chest proudly. He claimed to have fathered 31 sons, which made Danny wonder if the women in the village found it politic to routinely claim the chief as the father of their babies. As with all remote African villages, though, many children died of various sicknesses. Just a week earlier, one of the babies had succumbed to a terrible fever, the chief said.

The chief asked Danny the usual questions about his country, whether any black men lived there, why had he visited Cameroon; then he insisted that Danny eat dinner with them. The women would prepare the village's specialty of chicken in peanut sauce.

Hearing this, the old sentry emerged with his cutlass, smiled widely at Danny, then turned around the side wall. The squawking of a terrified chicken erupted in the sleepy afternoon air, the sounds of a scuffle, and then the squawking stopped.

Finally, Danny asked the question that had brought him to Kabas in the first place. *"Moi, je suis musicien; je cherche les tambours speciaux."* He mimed rapping on a small drum, then turned to Anatole for assistance.

The chief sat up startled, then nodded. He hammered on the air, mimicking drum playing, as if to make sure. Danny nodded. The chief clapped his hands and gestured for Anatole to take Danny somewhere. The boy pulled Danny to his feet and, surrounded by other chattering boys, dragged him back out of the walled courtyard. Danny managed to turn around and bow to the chief.

After trooping up a stair-like terrace of rock, they entered the courtyard of another homestead. The main shelter was made of hand-shaped blocks with a flat roof of corrugated metal. Anatole explained that this was the home of the local *sorcier*, or wizard.

Anatole called out, then gestured for Danny to follow through the low doorway. Inside the hut, the walls were hung with evidence of the *sorcier's* trade— odd bits of metal, small carvings, bundles of fur and feathers, mortars full of powders and herbs, clay urns for water and millet beer, smooth skins curing from the roof poles. And drums.

"*Tambours!*" Anatole said, spreading his hands wide.

Judging from the craftsman's tools around the hut, the *sorcier* made the village's drums as well as stored them. Danny saw several small gourd drums, larger log drums, and hollow cylinders of every size, all intricately carved with serpentine symbols, circles feeding into spirals, lines tangled into knots.

Danny reached out to touch one—then the *sorcier* himself stood up from the shadows near the far wall. Danny bit off a startled cry as the lithe old man glided forward. The *sorcier* was tall and rangy, but his skin was a battleground of wrinkles, as if someone had clumsily fashioned him out of papier-mâché.

"Pardon," Danny said. The wrinkled man had been sitting on a low stool, putting the finishing touches to a new drum.

Fixing his eyes on his visitor, the *sorcier* withdrew a medium-sized drum from a niche in the wall. Closing his eyes, he tapped on it. The mud walls of the hut reverberated with the hollow vibration, an earthy, primal beat that resonated in Danny's bones. Danny grinned with awe. Yes! The gaunt man's drum had not been a fluke. The drums

of Kabas had some special construction that caused this hypnotic tone.

Danny reached out tentatively. The wrinkled man gave him an appraising look, then extended the drum enough for Danny to strike it. He tapped a few tentative beats and laughed out loud when the instrument rewarded him with the same rich sound.

The *sorcier* turned away, taking the drum with him and returning it to its niche in the wall. In two flowing strides, the wrinkled man went to his stool in the shadows, picking up the drum he had been fashioning, moving it into the crack of light that seeped through the windows. Pointing, he spoke in a staccato dialect, which Anatole translated into pidgin French.

The *sorcier* is finishing a new drum today, Anatole said. Perhaps they would play it this evening, an initiation. The chief's baby son would have enjoyed that. From the baby's body, the *sorcier* had been able to salvage only enough skin to make this one small drum.

"What?" Danny said, looking down at the deep brown skin covering the top of the drum.

Anatole explained, as if it was the most ordinary thing in the world, that whenever one of the chief's many sons died, the *sorcier* used his skin to make one of Kabas's special drums. It had always been done.

Danny wrestled with that for a moment. On his first trip to Africa five years earlier, he had learned the wrenching truth of how different these cultures were.

"Why?" he finally asked. *"Pourquoi?"*

He had seen other drums made entirely of human skin taken from slain enemies, fashioned in the shape of stunted bodies with gaping mouths; when tapped a hollow sound came from the effigy's mouths. He knew that trying to impose his Western moral framework on the inhabitants of an alien land was hopeless. I'm sorry, sir, but you'll have to check your preconceptions at the door, he thought jokingly to himself.

"Magique." Anatole's eyes showed a flash of fear—fear born of respect for great power, rather than paranoia or panic. With the magic drums of Kabas, the chief could conquer any man, steal his heartbeat. It was old magic, a technique the village wizards had discovered long before the French had come to Cameroon, and before them the Germans. Kabas had been isolated, and at peace for longer than the memories of the oldest people in the village. Because of the drums. Anatole smiled, proud of his story, and Danny restrained an urge to pat him on the head.

Trying not to let his disbelief show, Danny nodded deeply to the *sorcier*. "*Merci,*" he said. As Anatole led him back out to the courtyard, the *sorcier* returned to his work on the small drum.

Danny wondered if he should have tried to buy one of the drums from the wrinkled man. Did he believe the story about using human skins? Probably. Why would Anatole lie?

As they left the *sorcier's* homestead to begin the trek back to the village, he looked westward across the jagged landscape of inselbergs. At sunset, the air filled with hundreds of kites, their wings rigid, circling high on the last thermals. Like leaves before the wind, the birds came spiraling down to disappear into the trees, filling them with the invisible flapping of wings.

When they reached the main village again, Danny saw that the women had returned from their labor in the nearby fields. He was familiar with the African tradition of sending the women and children out for backbreaking labor while the men lounged in the shade and talked "business."

The numerous sons of the chief and other adults gathered inside the courtyard near the fire, which the old sinewy woman had stoked into a larger blaze. Other men emerged, and Danny wondered where they had been hiding all afternoon. Out hunting? If so, they had nothing to show for their efforts. Anatole directed Danny to sit on a mat beside the chief, and everyone smiled vigorously at each other, the villagers exchanging the call-and-response litany of ritual greetings, which could go on for several minutes.

The old woman served the chief first, then the honored guest. She placed a brown yam like a baked potato on the mat in front of him, miming that it was hot. Danny took a cautious bite; the yam was pungent and turned to paste in his mouth. Then the woman reappeared with the promised chicken in peanut sauce. They ate quietly in a circle around the fire, ignoring each other, as red shadows flickered across their faces.

Listening to the sounds of eating, as well as the simmering evening hush of the West African hills, Danny felt the emptiness like a peaceful vacuum, draining away stress and loud noises and hectic schedules. After too many head-pounding tours and adrenaline-crazed performances, Danny was convinced he had forgotten how to sit quietly, how to slow down. After one rough segment of the last Blitzkrieg tour, he had taken a few days to go camping in the mountains; he recalled pacing in vigorous circles around the picnic table, muttering to himself that he was relaxing as fast as he could! Calming down was an acquired skill, he felt, and there was no better teacher than Africa.

After the meal, heads turned in the firelight, and Danny looked up to see the *sorcier* enter the chief's compound. The wrinkled man cradled several of his mystical drums. He placed one of the drums in front of the chief, then set the others on an empty spot on the ground. He squatted behind one drum, thrusting his long, lean legs up and to the side like the wings of a vulture.

Danny perked up. "A concert?" He turned to Anatole, who spoke rapidly to the *sorcier*. The wrinkled man looked skeptically at Danny, then shrugged. He picked up one of the extra drums and ceremoniously extended it to Danny.

Danny couldn't stop smiling. He took the drum and looked at it. The coffee-colored skin felt smooth and velvety as he touched it. A shiver went up his spine as he tapped the drumhead. Making music from human skin. He forced his instinctive revulsion back into the gray static of his mind, the place where he

stored things "to think about later." For now, he had the drum in his hands.

The chief thumped out a few beats, then stopped. The *sorcier* mimicked them and glanced toward Danny. "Jam session!" he muttered under his breath, then repeated the sequence easily and cleanly, but added a quick, complicated flourish to the end.

The chief raised his eyebrows, followed suit with the beat, and made it more complicated still. The *sorcier* flowed into his part, and Danny joined in with another counterpoint. It reminded him of the "Dueling Banjos" sequence from *Deliverance*.

The echoing, rich tone of the drum made his fingers warm and tingly, but he allowed himself to be swallowed up in the mystic rhythms, the primal pounding out in the middle of the African wilderness. The other night noises vanished around him, the smoke from the fire rose straight up, and the light centered into a pinpoint of his concentration.

Using his bare fingers—sticks would only interrupt the magical contact between himself and the drum—Danny continued weaving into their rhythms, trading points and counterpoints. The beat touched a core of past lives deep within him, an atavistic, pagan intensity, as the three drummers reached into the Pulse of the World. The chief played on; the *sorcier* played on; and Danny let his eyes fade half-closed in a rhythmic trance, as they explored the wordless language and hypnotic interplay of rhythm.

Danny became aware of the other boys standing up and swaying, jabbering excitedly and laughing as they danced around him. He deciphered their words as "White man drum! White man drum!" It was a safe bet they'd never seen a white man play a drum before.

Suddenly the *sorcier* stopped, and within a beat the chief also quit playing. Danny felt wrenched out of the experience, but reluctantly played a concluding figure as well, ending with an emphatic flam. His arms burned from the exertion, sweat dripped down the stubble on his chin. His ears buzzed from the noise. Unable to restrain himself, Danny began laughing with delight.

The *sorcier* said something, which Anatole translated. *"Vous avez l'esprit de batteur."* You have the spirit of a drummer.

With a throbbing hand, Danny squeezed Anatole's bare shoulder and nodded. *"Oui."*

The chief also congratulated him, thanking him for sharing his white man's music with the village. Danny found that ironic, since he had come here to pick up a rich African flavor for his compositions. But Danny could record his impressions in new songs; the village of Kabas had no way of keeping what he had brought to them.

The withered *sorcier* picked up one of the drums at his side, and Danny recognized it as the small drum the old man had been finishing in the dim hut that afternoon. He fixed his deep gaze on Danny for a moment, then handed it to him.

Anatole sat up, alarmed, but bit off a comment he had intended to make. Danny nodded in reassurance and in delight he took the new drum. He held it to his chest and inclined his head deeply to show his appreciation. *"Merci!"*

Anatole took Danny's hand to lead him away from the walled courtyard. The chief clapped his hands and barked something to the other boys, who looked at Anatole with glee before they got up and scurried to the huts for sleeping. Anatole stared nervously at Danny, but Danny didn't understand what had just occurred.

He repeated his thanks, bowing again to the chief and *sorcier*, but the two of them just stared at him. He was reminded of an East African scene: a pair of lions sizing up their prey. He shook his head to clear the morbid thought and followed Anatole.

DRUMBEATS

In the village proper, one of the round thatched huts had been swept for Danny to sleep in. Outside, his bicycle leaned against a tree, no doubt guarded during the day by the little man with the enormous cutlass. Anatole seemed uneasy, wanting to say something, but afraid.

Trying to comfort him, Danny opened his pack and withdrew a stick of chewing gum for the boy. Anatole spoke rapidly, gushing his thanks. Other boys suddenly materialized from the shadows with childish murder in their eyes. They tried to take the gum from Anatole, but he popped it in his mouth and ran off. "Hey!" Danny shouted, but Anatole bolted into the night with the boys chasing after.

Wondering if Anatole was in any real danger, Danny removed the blanket and sleeping bag from his bike, then carried them inside the guest hut. He decided the boy could take care of himself, that he had spent his life as the whipping boy for the other sons of the chief. The thought drained some of the exhilaration from the memory of the evening's performance.

His legs ached after the torturous ride upland from Garoua, and he fantasized briefly about sitting in the Jacuzzi in the capital suite of some five-star hotel.

He considered how wonderful it would be to sip on some cold champagne, or a scotch on the rocks.

Instead, he lifted the gift drum, inspecting it. He would find some way to use it on the next album, add a rich African tone to the music. Paul Simon and Peter Gabriel had done it, though the style of Blitzkrieg's music was a bit more … aggressive.

He would not tell anyone about the human skin, especially the customs officials. He tried without success to decipher the mystical swirling patterns carved into the wood, the interwoven curves, circles, and knots. It made him dizzy.

Danny closed his eyes and began to play the drum, quietly so as not to disturb the other villagers. But as the sound reached his ears, he snapped his eyes open. The tone from the drum was flat and weak, like a cheap tourist tom-tom, plastic over a coffee can.

He frowned at the gift drum. Where was the rich reverberation, the primal pulse of the earth? He tapped again, but heard only an empty and hollow sound, soulless. Danny scowled, wondering if the *sorcier* had ruined the drum by accident, then decided to get rid of it by giving it to the unsuspecting White Man who wouldn't know the difference.

Angry and uneasy, Danny set the African drum next to him; he would try it again in the morning. He could play it for the chief, show him its flat tone. Perhaps they would exchange it. Maybe he would have to buy another one.

He hoped Anatole was all right.

Danny sat down to pull the thorns and prickers from his clothes. The village women had provided him with two plastic basins of water for bathing, one for soaping and scrubbing, the other for rinsing. The warm water felt refreshing on his face, his neck. After stripping off his pungent socks, he rinsed his toes and soles.

The night stillness was hypnotic, and as he spread his sleeping bag and stretched out on it, he felt as if he were seeping into the cloth, into the ground, swallowed up in sleep....

Anatole woke him up only a few moments later, shaking him and whispering harshly in his ear. Dirt, blood, and bruises covered the boy's wiry body, and his clothes had been torn in a scuffle. He didn't seem to care. He kept shaking Danny.

But it was already too late.

Danny sat up, blinking his eyes. Sharp pains like a bear trap ripped through his chest. A giant hand had wrapped around his torso and would squeeze until his ribs popped free of his spine.

He gasped, opening and closing his mouth, but could not give voice to his agony. He grabbed Anatole's withered arm, but the boy struggled away, searching for something. Black spots swam in his eyes. He tried to breathe, but his chest wouldn't let him. He began slipping, sliding down an endless cliff into blackness.

Anatole finally reached an object on the floor of the hut. He snatched it up with his good hand, tucked it firmly under his withered arm, and began to thump on it.

The drum!

As the boy rapped out a slow, steady beat, Danny felt the iron band loosen around his heart. Blood rushed into his head again, and he drew a deep breath. Dizziness continued to swim around him, but the impossible pain receded. He clutched his chest, rubbing his sternum. He uttered a breathy thanks to Anatole.

Had he just suffered a heart attack? Good God, all the fast living had decided to catch up to him while he was out in the middle of nowhere, far from any hope of medical attention!

Then he realized with a chill that the sounds from the gift drum were now rich and echoey, with the unearthly depth he remembered from the other drums. Anatole continued his slow rhythm, and suddenly Danny recognized it. A heartbeat.

What was it the boy had told him inside the *sorcier's* hut—that the magical drums could steal a man's heartbeat? *"Ton coeur c'est dans ici,"* Anatole said, continuing his drumming. Your heartbeat lives in here now.

Danny remembered the gaunt, shambling man in the marketplace of Garoua, obsessively tapping the drum from Kabas as if his life depended on it, until his hide-wrapped fingers were bloodied. Had that man also escaped his fate in the village, and fled south?

"You had the spirit of a drummer," Anatole said in his pidgin French, "and now the drum has your spirit." As if to emphasize his statement, as if he knew a White Man would be skeptical of such magic, Anatole ceased his rhythm on the drum.

The claws returned to Danny's heart, and the vise in his chest clamped back down. His heart had stopped beating. Heart beats, drumbeats—

The boy stopped only long enough to convince Danny, then started the beat again. He looked with pleading eyes in the shadowy hut. *"Je vais avec toi!"* I go with you. Let me be your heartbeat. From now on.

Leaving his sleeping bag behind, Danny staggered out of the guest hut to his bicycle resting against an acacia tree. The rest of the village was dark and silent, and the next morning they would expect to find him dead and cold on his blankets; and the new drum would have the same resonant quality, the same throbbing of a captured spirit, to add to their collection. The sound of White Man's music for Kabas.

"*Allez!*" Anatole whispered as Danny climbed aboard his bike. Go! What was he supposed to do now? The boy ran in front of him along the narrow track. Danny did not fear navigating the rugged trail by moonlight, with snakes and who-knows-what abroad in the grass, as much as he feared staying in Kabas and being there when the chief and the *sorcier* came to look at his body in the morning, and no doubt to appraise their pale new drum skin.

But how long could Anatole continue his drumming? If the beat stopped for only a moment, Danny would seize up. They would have to take turns sleeping. Would this nightmare continue after he had left the vicinity of the village? Distance had not helped the shambling man in the marketplace in Garoua.

Would this be the rest of his life?

Stricken with panic, Danny nodded to the boy, just wanting to be out of there and not knowing what else to do. *Yes, I'll take you with me. What other choice do I have?* He pedaled his bike away from Kabas, crunching on the rough dirt path. Anatole jogged in front of him, tapping on the drum.

And tapping.

And tapping.

AFTERWORD: STORIES THAT FIRED MY IMAGINATION

NEIL PEART

IN THE LATE '80S, A NOVEL CALLED *RESURRECTION, Inc.* arrived in my mailbox, accompanied by a letter from the author, Kevin J. Anderson. He wrote that the book had been partly inspired by an album called

Grace Under Pressure, which my Rush bandmates and I had released in 1984.

It took me a year or so to get around to reading *Resurrection, Inc.*, but when I did, I was powerfully impressed, and wrote back to Kevin to tell him so. Any inspiration from Rush's work seemed indirect, at best, but nonetheless, Kevin and I had much in common, not least a shared love since childhood for science fiction and fantasy stories.

We began to write to each other occasionally, and during Rush's *Roll the Bones* tour in 1991, on a day off between concerts in California, I rode my bicycle from Sacramento to Kevin's home in Dublin, California. That was the beginning of a good friendship, many stimulating conversations (mostly by letter and e-mail, as we lived far apart), and regular packages in the mail, as we shared our latest work with each other—the ultimate stimulating conversation. In subsequent years I would send Kevin a few books of my own, numerous CDs and DVDs from my work with Rush, and there seemed to be a fat volume from Kevin arriving about every other month.

Back in 1991, though, Kevin was still working full-time as a technical writer at the Lawrence Livermore National Laboratory. He spent every spare minute working on his fiction, and though he would famously collect over 750 rejection letters, there was no doubt in Kevin's mind about his destiny. Even as a child, Kevin didn't "want to be" a writer when he grew up; he was *going to be* a writer.

And so he was. To date, Kevin has published over 80 novels, story collections, graphic novels, and comic books, and he still spends every minute *being a writer*. Kevin doesn't write to live, he lives to write.

He has even found ways to weave his recreation, relaxation, and desire for adventure and physical challenge into the writing process, carrying a microcassette recorder on long hikes throughout the West, including the ascent of each of Colorado's 46 "fourteeners," (peaks over 14,000 feet).

In a recent exchange of e-mails, Kevin and I were discussing writing styles and habits, and he offered this revealing passage:

> A long time ago, my friend and collaborator Doug Beason made a joking comment when I suggested that I needed a break, a sabbatical. He said, "Kevin, if you ever stop writing, your head would explode!"

And I knew he was right. My imagination is stuck in overdrive, for better or worse. Instead of a writer calling for a Muse to give him an idea, I've got a hyperactive Muse that won't leave me alone.

I feel as if my head is a pot filled with too many popcorn kernels, popping away, filling the container and pushing the lid up, and unless I keep shoveling the new stuff out, the whole thing will blow up on me. I'm writing as fast as I can to keep the growling, slavering Ideas from nipping too close at my heels.

There was a *US News & World Report* article a few months ago about a newly "found" disease they called "hypergraphia," the compulsion to write. They said writers like Sylvia Plath and Tolstoy were so obsessed with writing they often wrote as much as a thousand words a day. (A thousand words? Man, I've done over 10,000 words in a day!) I guess I'm an addict.

I'm picturing you as a guy with a similar compulsion to drum, slapping your knees, the furniture, the walls, feeling a rhythm in your blood. It's what you do. For me, stories are the

DRUMBEATS

drumbeats inside me. I'm always fabricating stories, characters, weird locations, plot twists. I'm just not happy "relaxing." Sometimes I'm just banging around having fun, goofing with toys that I enjoy—as when I write Star Wars or comics or light books like *Sky Captain*; other times I'm intense and working on something I think is Really Important, like *Hopscotch*. The "Seven Suns" books are a little of both, the biggest and most challenging story I've ever told, but damn, I'm having the time of my life with it too.

I've been saying for years and years, "soon I'll slow down and take more time to smell the roses." It'll never happen, I suppose, because I just love the writing so much. Three days ago, I started writing Seven Suns #5, and I was in absolute euphoria plotting the 112 chapters. This happens, then this happens, then this happens—I was discovering what my beloved characters were going to do, where they would end up, who would die, who would triumph. I came up with some twists and new ideas that were revelations to me, real lightning bolts from the hyperactive

Muse—and best of all, they were so *logical* and *inevitable* in the universe of the story, that it seemed as if they were sewn into the fabric of my imagination from the very beginning, but I just didn't realize it yet. Now that's cool.

So, yes, I would like to have that sense of stillness and the time to pay attention deeply to the things around me ... but on the other hand, I can't wait to see what happens next in the new novel that's just over the horizon.

And Kevin Anderson's horizons are wider than most—infinite, really. His imagination roams the entire universe, creating strange new worlds and peopling them with strong, believable characters.

From the philosophical depth of *Resurrection, Inc.* and *Hopscotch*, to the novelizations for *Star Wars* and *The X-Files;* from the genre of "historical fantasy" (which I think Kevin *invented*—richly-imagined tales about Jules Verne, H.G. Wells, and Charles Dickens), to the breathtaking scope of his "imagineering" in the Seven Suns series, there have been so many excellent works that have delighted *this* reader, and millions of others.

DRUMBEATS

Among seemingly overlooked treasures, I fondly remember the fantasy trilogy, *Gamearth*, *Gameplay*, and *Game's End*, but there are also Kevin's collaborations with Doug Beason, like *The Trinity Paradox* and *Ill Wind*, and the ongoing, highly successful Dune series with Brian Herbert.

In writing to Kevin in response to reading one of those, *The Butlerian Jihad*, I talked about the subtle skill of his craft:

> More and more I notice how truly masterful writing, yours and others', leaves the reader with an overall impression of making it all seem *easy*—regardless of how much work has gone into the craft, the background, the research, and the intellectual underpinnings (or maybe *because* of all that), it just breathes off the page in a smooth flow of seemingly-inevitable revelations.
>
> I know I've made similar comments about drummers before: some of them try to make simple things look difficult and impressive, but the true masters make the impossible seem easy.
>
> It doesn't seem fair to the *creator* of that carefully wrought illusion, undermining all

the effort and experience necessary to operate at that rarefied level, but it's the ultimate nature of mastery, I guess. (It may be lonely at the top, but it must feel better than being at the bottom!)

In late 2002, toward the end of a long American tour that had me drained and feeling sorry for myself, I wrote to Kevin:

> One bright spot I can report along the way is that during some idle hours in the tuning room, on the bus, and in hotel rooms, I had the great pleasure of reading *Hidden Empire*.
> First of all, I have to tell you that if you or anyone else had any doubt, I think you have achieved a true Masterpiece with this book—meaning that term in the sense which *you* clarified for me years ago. It is definitely a piece of work to lay alongside those of the Masters, to be accepted by them and by the great abstraction of "the Audience" as one of the pantheon of masters yourself.
> Congratulations. I really think it is a great book. I was so impressed by it at the

time, and also after the fact—a true test of quality, I'm sure you'll agree.

The craftsmanship alone is sheer perfection. The architecture of the storytelling moves forward with grace and economy, combining girders and panels of deft characterizations, wondrous settings, admirable "imagineering," and all the superstructure of pure *thought* that has preceded all that.

(The reader will have observed by now that when Kevin asked me to write this essay, it was easy to say yes—I knew the important stuff had already been written, either by me or by him. I would only have to look it up!)

Here are some of Kevin's thoughts on "style," from a recent exchange of e-mails on the subject:

> I think in a letter to you many years ago, I talked about creating believable worlds and scenes; one of the vital tricks I mentioned was to nail down a few small but very precise and mundane details (the color of a piece of lint, the brand of a gum wrapper wadded up in a gutter), and the reader will buy into the

rest of what you're describing. It seems easy, seems transparent. It's simple to show off, to be flashy and flamboyant, to prance around and point at marvelous overblown metaphors. It's more difficult to be subtle.

To which I replied, in part:

Another note about writing style that occurred to me in connection with what I wrote the other day: I just finished Gabriel García Márquez's memoir, *Living to Tell the Tale*, and he described his early decision as a writer to avoid all adverbs of the "ly" sort *(mento* in Spanish, I think), and how it became almost pathological with him, just as Hemingway tried to cut every unnecessary adjective.

In your case, with the necessary "mission" of describing an entirely imaginary universe for the reader, it would seem especially difficult to avoid extraneous adjectives and adverbs—and yet you *do*, making the descriptions of planets, cities, palaces, customs, and technology fall more-or-less naturally into the ongoing narrative. And ... you make it look so *easy*.

As we have discussed, that is the highest level of craft, and yet the least likely to be admired, or even appreciated. Once I offered a definition of genius, in particular reference to Buddy Rich: "Doing the impossible, and making it look easy."

And yes, Kevin does make it look easy, though of course it's not. He works to a very high standard of quality in his writing, from the conception to the execution, and these stories are a testament to the consistency of his art.

When people have called him lucky, Kevin likes to counter, "Yes, and the harder I work, the luckier I get."

As one of his appreciative readers, I think the harder Kevin works, the luckier *we* get.

—Neil Peart

"The measure of a life is a measure of love and respect."
—Neil Peart, "The Garden"

ABOUT THE AUTHORS

Photo by T. Duren Jones

KEVIN J. ANDERSON is the bestselling science-fiction author of 165 novels. His original works include the Saga of Seven Suns series; *Spine of the Dragon*; the Terra Incognita trilogy; and with Brian Herbert, is the co-author of 15 novels in the Dune universe. He has written spin-off novels for *Star Wars*, DC Comics, and *The X-Files*. His first novel, *Resurrection, Inc.*, was inspired by the Rush album *Grace Under Pressure*, with lyrics by Neil Peart.

Photo by Kelly Drew

NEIL PEART is the drummer and lyricist of the legendary rock band Rush and the author of *Ghost Rider*, *The Masked Rider*, *Traveling Music*, *Roadshow*, *Far and Away*, *Far and Near*, and *Far and Wide*.

ANDERSON AND PEART coauthored the steampunk fantasy novels *Clockwork Angels* and *Clockwork Lives*, as well as graphic novel adaptations of both, and the story "Drumbeats."

Neil Peart passed away January 2020 after a long battle with brain cancer.

ABOUT THE ARTIST

Photo by Andrée-Anne Séguin

STEVE OTIS is an accomplished comic artist, illustrator, sculptor, and teacher. He started to draw at a very early age, fueled by images of DC and Marvel comics, and then the great Warren magazines (Creepy and Eerie in the early 70s). From there he began to delve more deeply into horror, gothic and sci fi art. Heavily influenced by Frazetta, Boris and Richard Corben, he did extensive fantasy work in the late nineties for collectible card games. By the early 2000s, he began to look for techniques to challenge his artistic style in a more "Fine Art" vein while keeping firmly to the themes of dark art.

Steve graduated from the Laval University of Quebec with a major in Art Teaching. He taught art in high school for ten years before concentrating on painting. He has participated in many solo exhibitions and collective art shows in Quebec, Montreal, Italy and a few states in the USA.

He discovered Rush in 1979 with *Hemispheres*. The words of Neil Peart resounded on my heartstrings, from his trippy sci fi lyrics of the late seventies to the worldview lyrics of his recent works. Neil's astonishing drumming made Steve an amazingly inept air drummer at over 17 Rush concerts from 1981–2015. It is his great honor and privilege to take part in this project.

ACKNOWLEDGMENTS

This story was written a long time ago, and we never imagined it would still be around decades later. I'm so glad to see it have a new life.

These are just my own, Kevin's, acknowledgments, and even though he is my coauthor, I cannot express enough gratitude to Neil Peart, not only for this story but for all the memories we shared, all the inspiration he gave me, and the ideas I will never forget.

And to my wife Rebecca Moesta, whom Neil called "a great partner for an obsessive writer" (and he's right!), who has helped to improve not only this story but all my writing. And Neil's wife Carrie and daughter Olivia.

Steve Otis, brilliant artist, stepped up to the plate without even being asked to create this gorgeous volume. Allyson Longueira created the interior layout to let the story shine. Janet McDonald did the wonderful cover design.

And finally, a special thanks to the whole Rush family who showed such tremendous support, love, and gratitude in a difficult time, Love and respect to all of you.

—KJA

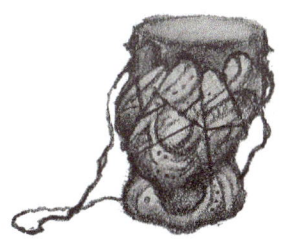

IF YOU LIKED DRUMBEATS YOU MAY ALSO LIKE

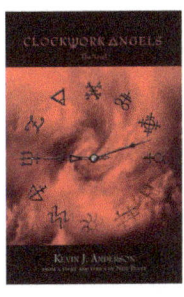

Clockwork Angels
by Kevin J. Anderson
and Neil Peart

Clockwork Lives
by Kevin J. Anderson
and Neil Peart

Resurrection, Inc.
by Kevin J. Anderson

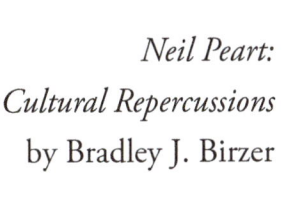

*Neil Peart:
Cultural Repercussions*
by Bradley J. Birzer

Printed in the USA
CPSIA information can be obtained
at www.ICGtesting.com
CBHW070810130824
12946CB00052B/253/J